Also by the author

Like Fire Unbound
English Arcadia
The Damnation of Peter Pan
The Last Good Man

JACK AND BARRY

SIMON PETHERICK

JACK
AND
BARRY

SIMON PETHERICK

Leapfrog Press
New York and London

Jack and Barry
9 8 7 6 5 4 3 2 1

First published in the United States by Leapfrog Press, 2023

Leapfrog Press Inc.
www.leapfrogpress.com

First published in the United Kingdom by TSB, 2023

TSB is an imprint of:
Can of Worms Enterprises Ltd
7 Peacock Yard, London SE17 3LH
www.canofworms.net

© 2023 Simon Petherick

Cover and text design: James Shannon
Set in ITC American Typewriter

ISBN: 978-1-948585-675 (Paperback)
ISBN: 978-1-911673-385 (Hardback)

To Tamsin

Jack and Barry

It's just after six o'clock on Saturday evening on December 5, 1964, and Barry Goldwater is driving a light blue Buick Riviera south down State Route 69 towards his home in Paradise Valley, just north of Phoenix, Arizona. Barry has had quite a tumultuous year: a month ago, he lost the Presidential Election to Lyndon B Johnson by one of the biggest margins in American electoral history. Back in June, he upset a lot of people by voting against the Civil Rights Bill on the floor of the Senate despite his lifelong active support of desegregation

in his home state of Arizona; he believes
government should stay out of peoples' lives
as much as possible. On top of that, he can't
stand for re-election as one of Arizona's two
Senators next month, because he had to forfeit
that bid in order to stand for the Presidency.
In the space of a few months, he's become one
of the most vilified politicians in America and
he's out of a job. Barry is fifty-five years old
and he's just spent two days photographing
landscapes around the Hohokam villages near
Lake Pleasant.

SR 69 isn't a great road and the big Buick's
suspension rolls and heaves with the dips and
potholes. He's about ten miles north of the
Valley and over to the west beyond Glendale he
can see the sun begin its descent below White
Tank Mountain. Pretty soon he'll need to take
a left fork off the highway and head in towards
home. The road is quiet but up ahead on the
other side of the road, maybe two hundred

yards away, he sees a figure walking in the
dust track beside the oncoming lane. Late to be
out walking this time of year, he thinks.

Once he's passed, Barry pulls the car across
the highway over to the other side and rolls
the wheels off the tarmac. He looks in the rear
view mirror and can see the figure approaching
in the evening light. He's walking in a kind of
loping but steady way. Barry rolls down the
window and looks back down the track.

'Hey fella, you need a lift into town? Getting
kind of late out here.'

The walker approaches. He's stocky, maybe
5-foot-eight or nine, wearing what looks like a
seaman's blue sweater and he's got a leather
bag swung over his shoulder. His workman's
jeans are dusty, his brown boots are dirty
with dried mud. He has dark black hair and
as he stops beside the car, Barry takes in the
swarthy complexion, the clenched cheekbones,
the thick dark eyebrows.

'I'm heading northwest of the Valley,' Barry
continues as the stranger stays silent. 'Near to
that new Methodist church they're building.'

The guy nods.

'I know it,' he says. 'I do some work for
them.'

'You heading my way?' Barry asks.

The man shrugs.

'Kind of. I'm the other side of the mountain,
Hummingbird Lane.'

'I know it. I'll drop you there, you're not far
out of my way.'

The guy nods and walks around the front
of the car, lets himself into the passenger seat.
There's a skittering of stones as Barry gets
the Buick back up onto the highway and they
cruise on towards Phoenix.

Barry turns his head, his thick black-
rimmed glasses flashing the evening sun which
has cast his passenger into shade.

'What are you, Mexican?' he asks.

The guy looks at him for a moment, then nods.

'Thought I spotted the accent,' Barry says. 'Had a great time down there last year.' He takes his right hand off the wheel and extends it. 'Barry Goldwater,' he says.

Again, the fellow hesitates, then he reaches out to grip.

'Juan Abatido,' he says.

'What do you do for the Methodists, Juan?'

Another pause.

'I look after their garden. I'm a gardener.'

'Oh. Peggy – that's my wife – she's been looking for a gardener. Maybe you've got some spare hours?'

'Maybe.'

'OK, we'll see. It's not so easy finding a gardener, she tells me. Where in Mexico you from?'

Juan waits for a second, then,

'The City.'

'Down south, huh? Long way. Took Peggy to Mexico City for our honeymoon, thirty damn years ago. Stayed in the Ritz.' He chuckles. 'Not that I remember much of it.'

After a moment's silence, Barry peers at the man once more and says,

'Say, you got something else in you? Some American? You look as though you might. I'm half Jewish, if you want to know. We're all half of something and half of something else, I guess.'

'My mom was French Canadian, her family was from Brittany in France.'

Barry nods.

'Thought so. Your parents back in Mexico?'

Juan shakes his head.

'No, they're both dead now.'

'I'm sorry to hear that,' says Barry. 'I apologize for butting in.'

'No apology,' says Juan. 'They did OK.'

'You're young though, to lose both your parents.'

'Am I? How old are you?'

Barry laughs. 'I'm fifty-five, I'm what you call a genuine oldtimer. You're, what, mid forties?'

'You're an inquisitive gentleman, Mr. Goldwater.'

'Barry, call me Barry.' He laughs again. 'Peggy says there's no anthill I won't go poke my goddamn nose into.'

'She sounds OK, your wife.'

'Oh that she is, that she is. You got one?'

'No, sir.'

Barry looks at him again.

'Say, what are you doing out here walking along the highway this time of year, anyhow?'

'Been out hiking a couple of days.'

Barry nods. 'That's just fine,' he says. 'We have the world's finest hiking lands here in this state of Arizona. You got yourself a bedroll in there?'

'And a skillet and a knife. And an old copy

of the *Diamond Sutra* which I didn't read.'

'Say what?'

'The *Diamond Sutra*. It's a Buddhist text.'

'Well now you do surprise me, Juan. A half-Mexican, half-French Canadian, Buddhist gardener. I'll wager there aren't so many like you in Paradise Valley or back in Mexico City, for that matter.'

Barry would be more surprised if he knew that his passenger wasn't really called Juan Abatido but was in fact Jack Kerouac, author of *On The Road*. Jack's been using the name Abatido since he's been in Paradise Valley the last four weeks. He's in the Valley incognito with his typewriter, trying to start another novel. He's rented a tiny adobe hut the other side of Mummy Mountain from Barry's expansive ranch. He has no idea why he told Barry he was gardening for the Methodists but now he's taken by the idea of being a Mexican gardener. Maybe he could pursue that? He

came up with the name Juan Abatido as a
derivation of what his mother Gabrielle, or
Mémère as he calls her, uses for him: Ti Jean,
French for Little Jack. (Mémère, of course, is
very much alive and is expecting him to be
back home with her in St Petersburg, Florida,
for Christmas. His sister Nin died in Florida
just three months ago and of course he's
feeling guilty about not being with Mémère at
this time.) Abatido is Spanish for dejected or
low or, you know, beat. *On The Road* came out
seven years before and Jack is sick to the very
core of himself with the role of spokesman for
the Beat Generation that the newspapers and
TV have allotted him.

Barry turns left off State Route 69 onto West
Glendale Road, a long, rough track with just a
few houses scattered about, cactus and Joshua
trees thriving in the sandy ground. They pass
one house set back from the track which has
some Christmas illuminations in the window.

'You celebrate Christmas, Juan?' asks Barry.

'Sure,' says Jack.

'Peggy just loves Christmas,' Barry says, smiling again. 'We're going to have all four kids back home with us this year, and two grandchildren. Boy, oh boy, it's going to be a lulu.'

'You'll have to dress up as Santa, I guess?' Jack asks.

'Ho, ho, ho,' says Barry.

There's still just enough light for the car headlights to stay off and Barry's on East Lincoln Drive now.

'I can see the mountain,' he says, pointing. 'Where's your place?'

'You don't need to take me all the way there,' Jack says. 'Just drop me here, I can walk the rest.'

'No can do,' says Barry. 'I said I'd drop you home and that's what I'll do. Shall I take a left here?'

Jack nods and Barry swerves up onto a

dusty track that begins to incline rapidly. Jack points directions at a couple of forks in the track and then he says,

'It's this place,' looking towards a small, one-storey building surrounded by lemon trees. Barry pulls the car up and Jack lifts his leather bag out, steps out and leans back through the open passenger door window.

'Thanks for the lift,' he says.

'My pleasure, Juan,' says Barry. 'Here —' he pulls out a card from his wallet – 'this is my address. The house is called Be-Nun-I-Kin. Peggy wants the garden all smart before the kids come for Christmas. Will you call by tomorrow and see what you can do?'

Jack looks at the card.

'Sure,' he says. He looks back at Barry, who's smiling and getting ready to shift into reverse to head back down the hill. 'Tough luck on that election, Barry,' Jack says. And he turns and heads off towards the door of the little shack.

'Well, I'll be,' Barry says to himself as the Buick rumbles down the stone track. 'That's one interesting fellow.'

Jack opens the wooden door of the adobe hut and drops his bag on the floor. There's an unmade bed in one corner, a small gas stove next to a sink in another and a table set against one wall with a typewriter on it. At the back of the table is a neat stack of paper: the proof copies of *Desolation Angels* which he's supposed to be correcting; there are inches of foolscap sheets, his collected notes on Buddhism for the book which will come out much later, *Some of the Dharma*. On the floor is a cardboard box half-filled with bottles. He walks over to the table, reaches down and lifts a bottle of rye whiskey from the box, then heads back outside.

The hut faces towards the peak of Mummy Mountain and the evening sky now is a cold purple. There are no other houses around

here. Jack rented the place from an associate
of William Burroughs, his writer friend who's
currently living over in London, England.
Burroughs's wealthy family made their money
selling business machines, some of which were
built down in Tucson, and the family invested
in Paradise Valley when it started to grow in
the 1940s. One of the Burroughs associates, a
landowner called Charles Mieg, gave Mummy
Mountain its name in 1947 when he was trying
to sell plots of land in this new desert enclave.
He was toying with marketing ideas to attract
investors to this beautiful, empty Arizona
valley and one day he realised the mountain
looked like an Egyptian mummy lying down.

Jack sets the bottle of rye down on the
sand outside the shack and turns to face the
wall of the hut. He crouches down, puts his
head in his hands and jerks his legs up, slowly
straightening them until he's in a headstand,
his whole body one line up from the ground.

He's upside down, his heels touching the wall.
He's suffered from phlebitis most of his life,
a painful inflammation of his legs caused by
a sports injury at high school but probably
exacerbated by a lifetime of booze. Years ago,
when he was riding box cars in California, he
met an old hobo who told him if he stood on his
head once a day, his phlebitis would be eased
and he's been doing it ever since. Now his eyes
can follow the sand outside the house towards
the ridge overlooking the valley down below
and there are a few lights starting to show in
the ranches scattered about the valley floor.

He stays up for a few minutes then drops
his legs back to the ground, levers himself
up and sits back against the wall. He pulls
the cork out of the bottle and takes a swig
of whiskey — his first in two days. It's silent
high up here on the ridge, so quiet that some
nights he can hear the wings of the eagles as
they swoop over the tip of the mountain. Jack

wishes the silence would console him, would allow him to meditate upon the sutras, let his mind expand into the Arizona night, but it doesn't and hasn't since he's been here. All he has is noise in his head that he doesn't want to hear and he shuts that noise up every night with the rye whiskey and then once more he can soar with the eagles above the mountain and up towards the stars that are beginning to appear in the blackening sky.

Jack hasn't written anything in the four weeks he's been here and he wonders again why he just doesn't stop with the whole thing and forget he ever wanted to be the writer who would capture the soul of modern America. He takes another thick gulp of rye. Since *On The Road* finally came out seven years ago, he's had nine more books published: *The Subterraneans*, *The Dharma Bums*, *Doctor Sax*, *Maggie Cassidy*, *Tristessa*, *Lonesome Traveler*, *Book of Dreams*, *Big Sur* and *Visions of Gerard*.

To him, they're all part of one massive written
project, *The Legend of Duluoz*, to follow in the
footsteps of Walt Whitman and Thomas Wolfe
and bring the story of America up to date
in a language that honours the brilliance of
bebop jazz; to most of the critics and much of
the reading public, however, he's an illiterate
clown, falling down drunk on TV chat shows
and spouting incomprehensible stuff about
becoming bodhisattva. 'That's not writing,
that's typing,' sneered Truman Capote when
On The Road came out. He's made money from
the books but not that much, he's still living at
home with Mémère, his relations with Ginsberg
and Corso and Cassady are all busted and
he's constantly besieged by dumb college kids
wanting to talk about hitchhiking and bringing
him bottles of whiskey when he's trying to
stay off the juice. Jack loves his country just as
much as he hates himself and he despises all
the bullshit his friends espouse about socialism

and freedom and free love. Somewhere in the
earth and in the night sky and in the memories
of his youth in Lowell, Massachusetts and in
the notes of Charlie Parker there is the true
America which still eludes him. He came out
here to Arizona for one last attempt to put his
house in order, but all he's done is drink and be
sick and piss blood and sometimes the eagles
overhead look like vultures, circling over his
broken faith.

While Jack quietly slips once more into his
whiskey nirvana, Barry has his headphones
on in the ham radio room he built himself
at home and he's talking to an airfield flight
controller in northern Arizona. He's going to
fly up to Page on the border with Utah in a day
or two to oversee the final sale of the trading
post he's owned at Navajo Mountain for the
last twenty years, so he needs to book a spot
on the landing strip at the small airfield there.
From his desk littered with paper and electrical

equipment and the walls covered in dials and volt meters, he can see through the window over to the lights above Sky Harbor airport at Phoenix. Barry flew planes for his country during World War Two and he's still a Major General in the Army Air Reserve. He keeps his own twin-engine Bonanza at Sky which he uses to hop around the country giving his talks. Since last month, though, the demand for the talks has dropped.

Peggy comes into the room, slim and handsome and wearing a gingham apron. She sets down a martini beside the pad Barry's jotting in while he listens to the flight controller.

'Supper in fifteen minutes,' she whispers, kisses him on the forehead and goes back out again.

Half an hour later they're both sitting at a table beside another huge window which looks over towards Camelback Mountain, one of the other natural boundaries for the Valley. Peggy and Barry built Be-Nun-I-Kin in 1957, the same year Jack finally became famous with *On The Road*. It's a low, wide ranch set into the peak of Scorpion Hill, a sweeping modern structure built from the Arizona granite called schist and sandstone from one of the Navajo reservations; the name is a Navajo term for *House on the Hill*. The house was designed to afford views on all four sides across different aspects of their beloved Valley. They've got steak and baked potatoes and Barry's filling his wife's glass again with Napa red wine, telling her about the unusual fellow he gave a lift to.

'That's just fine, dear,' she says, cutting into the steak. 'If he's strong I'll get him to dig up a couple of the cacti so we can make a playpit for Carolyn.' Carolyn is the six-year-old daughter of their first child, Joanne, who will be coming to Be-Nun-I-Kin for Christmas with her husband, Thomas.

'Didn't look in great shape, though,' Barry

continues. 'Puffy face, blotchy.'

'I think some Mexicans like to drink just a little too much, darling,' says Peggy. 'I'll give him some nice homemade lemonade tomorrow.'

After dinner, while Peggy sits in the big lounge with the logs crackling in the cavernous open fire writing a letter to their eldest son, Barry is back in the radio room, logging into conversations with amateur radio operators. Barry's always liked technology; he's an irrepressible optimist about man's ability to create. In a few years' time, after Lyndon Johnson has sent hundreds and hundreds of thousands of young men to Vietnam, Barry's ham radio room will be used to help distraught American families make contact with their loved ones dying in the paddy fields. That's all to come, together with the unravelling of the Republican vision which Barry had attempted to set out in books like *Conscience of a Conservative* and at the stump over the last

year's campaigning. It will be almost twenty
years before Ronald Reagan holds aloft in
victory the baton that Barry passed him, but
by then Barry will have gone on record saying
such things as, 'What I see today in American
big business is absolutely revolting, disgusting
and frightening.' Throughout two terms, Reagan
never once invited Barry to the White House.

'Billy! Great to hear you! What's the weather
in Alaska?' Barry shouts into the mike as
Peggy seals her envelope in the room next door.

****

The next morning, Jack rinses the vomit out of
his mouth with the pail of water he's lifted up
from the well out back. The sun has risen up
over Camelback Mountain southeast from him
and he does a few stretches on the sand to get
his circulation moving after another cold night
in the cabin. He goes back inside, lights the gas

ring on the stove and throws the greasy skillet
on. He takes three eggs from a string basket
hanging from a nail on the wall and breaks
them into the skillet. The coffee that he put on
earlier is bubbling now on the next ring and
he tentatively grabs at the handle to check it's
not too hot. It's just OK, so he pours his first
cup of black coffee into a stained white enamel
mug. He sips it while he moves the eggs around
the butter in the pan. He picks up a spoon and
wanders back outside with the skillet and his
coffee, sits with his back against the wall of the
hut and scoops egg into his mouth, all the time
watching the flicker of cars moving over 2,000
feet down below in the valley. Jack's adobe hut
is probably two-thirds of the way up the mountain, it's one of the highest.

Apart from the old guy behind the counter
of the grocery store down in the town, Barry
Goldwater is the first person Jack has spoken
to since he arrived in Paradise Valley four

weeks ago. He and Mémère both voted for
Barry at the election and Jack was sore to see
that lying son of a bitch Johnson sweep in. Now
we're in for it. He'll lose more of his royalties
too, they're bound to raise taxes. Despite all
the press and TV hysteria over the last few
years, Jack still doesn't make that much out of
his writing but he makes enough now to have
been able to take the Douglas DC-8 from Tampa
to Phoenix, knocking back highballs as he
looked out the window over southern America,
and he hasn't stuck his thumb out at the side
of the road for years. The Democrats are going
to come for his money, that's for sure, and
what they don't take, his ex-wife Joan will grab
in the ongoing paternity suit he's been fighting.
But what really worries him is there's no more
juice in the tank: these last four weeks have
pretty much confirmed that. Nothing written
other than his usual flood of letters, weekly
reports in to Mémère, berating missives to

Ginsberg, Cassady, Corso, followed by shorter
apologies. He's the famous American writer
who can't write any more.

Perhaps he'll just be Juan Abatido for these
last two weeks. What did Barry call him? A
half-Canadian, half-Mexican Buddhist gardener.
That'll be just fine. He can spend his days with
his hands in the dry Arizona earth, better
that than wasting them lying motionless on
the silent typewriter keys. He sits with the
empty skillet on his lap and watches as two
heavy black crows land ungracefully the other
side of the road track and begin to dart their
beaks into what looks from where he's sitting
to be the carcass of a squirrel or a marmot.
Agitatedly, they dig away into the body but
then a bigger magpie flaps down over them,
scattering them and leaving the treat to
himself as he fixes the dead body to the sand
with one claw while he tugs at the flesh with
his beak until he finds an intestine which he

skilfully pulls out like a long string. Once he's got about two feet of it out, he rounds it up with his beak, clamps hold of it and flies off.

Jack walks back into the hut, clatters the skillet and mug into the sink, then stares at his reflection in the small round mirror on the wall. His face is heavy now, jowly with drink. His eyes have lost their sharp, blue, darting stare that used to take in all the faces at the jazz clubs in New York and all the hills of the Mid West and all the kids staring at him in the markets of Mexico City. Now they're tired and dark. Juan Abatido. How could he sit out here for four weeks and not write a damn thing? Only a couple of years ago he wrote *Big Sur* on a mix of benzedrine and marijuana down in Mexico City. He's always been able to write, that's the point of him. While the others stand up at poetry readings or go on anti-war marches or write damn nonsense in the *New York Times*, Jack has always just covered the pages with words, beautiful words that reach into the lungs of America. Ginsberg once said he was more writer than human. Now, nothing.

Maybe it's not him. Maybe his America is dying, dying in the same hospital bed as Woody Guthrie, the same limousine as Jack Kennedy. The America of steel and iron and earth and blood and sweat, of towering Californian pines, railroad tracks, camaraderie, love, truth. Maybe there's a new America coming which can never be lyrical again, which will barter safety for freedom, comfort for joy. There's nothing to say about this new America, Jack fears: it's dead from the waist down. Jack tries to talk about these things when he gets invited on fool TV shows like Ed Sullivan, when he's introduced for the thousandth time as the writer who invented the Beat Generation, and all he wants to talk about is how you don't need anything but the American earth and the American night sky and that will sustain you your whole life

and give you eternal beauty, but it never seems
to come out right and usually he's drunk and
the audience sniggers as he slips off his stool.

Jack Kerouac in 1964 is famous, you
see, famous in the way that rock stars like
Bob Dylan will be soon, which is a different
famous to the way Elvis and Sinatra were
famous before. Jack is a new kind of famous:
he's turned into the property of his readers
and of the people who don't read him but
read *about* him in the papers. He's become
Jack Kerouac, a kind of Disney beat poet who
seems to inspire people to believe that they
know him deeply, that he's their brother,
their husband, their best friend. He's literally
besieged by fans: some nights in St Petersburg,
he hears them clambering on the roof and
Mémère will call out from her room: 'Ti Jean,
Ti Jean, j'ai peur.' He's interrupted this guy
going through his garbage and the guy doesn't
back off, he confronts Jack about why he's

holed up in Florida when he should be on the
road gathering his people for the impending
Beat Revolution. There are vendors in Times
Square in New York selling Jack Kerouac
T-shirts and when Jack pitches up there for
one of his regular week-long booze missions he
finds himself playing the role of Jack Kerouac
in front of those T-shirt stands, grinning
drunkenly in photographs with kids draped
around him. With *On The Road*, Jack achieved
his life's ambition of becoming a famous
published writer but something different
happened with him; plenty of other writers
before him, from Hemingway on, sold plenty
and appeared everywhere in the press and on
TV, but Jack is the first writer who has really
become such an object of fantastical belief. If
we're talking numbers here, Barry has sold
more copies than Jack, since his 1960 book
Conscience of a Conservative has already sold
over two million copies, but Barry was never

turned into a degraded icon, he was always just
Barry Goldwater. Jack is the first truly famous
writer of the modern world.

But he doesn't want to be famous; he wants
to be truthful. That's why he chose Arizona
and Burroughs's cabin for this retreat: he
has no friends in Arizona, no one knows him
here. He thought he could write truthfully
here, but now he thinks no-one wants to be
truthful any more. Swift moving time has made
him redundant, pointless. What's the point of
singing songs, when no-one wants to listen?
Let's just go back to our garden, like Voltaire
said. Ti Jean will become Juan Abatido, and
he will go and dig the earth for Mr. and Mrs.
Barry Goldwater of Paradise Valley, Arizona.

An hour later, Jack has rounded the
upper slopes of Mummy Mountain and has
dropped down past the country club and onto
East Lincoln Drive, trudging along the sandy
road out west towards where he thinks the

Goldwaters live. He passes the Methodist
church he pretended to know about and he
stops to ask one of the construction workers
where Barry's house is.

'Keep going pal, take a left when you
see Scorpion Hill in about half a mile. Mr.
Goldwater's house is on the top.'

Sure enough, before too long he sees a
long, sleek building sitting atop a low hill off
East Lincoln Drive. There's flashes of sunlight
glancing off the huge windows of the single-
story ranch and a trail of woodsmoke curling
out one of the chimneys. Jack's pleased: that
looks like the kind of house Barry Goldwater
should live in. It's almost sculpted out of
the Arizona rock and there are few other
neighbouring houses in sight.

As he climbs the winding road up to the
gate, he sees a woman in the garden, a scarf
around her hair and a cigarette in one hand,
a cup of coffee in the other. She's watching his

slow progress up the hill. As he gets closer, she sets the cup down on the ground and walks across the tarmac driveway to open the gate.

'Hello,' she calls out brightly. 'I think you must be Juan.'

He stops the other side of the gate.

'Ma'am,' he says, holding his arms down at his sides.

'Barry told me all about you, Juan,' she continues. 'I'm so glad you've come. I want to make the garden just dandy in time for Christmas. Come along in, I've got some homemade lemonade for you before we start.'

Jack's positively enjoying himself. Barry Goldwater's wife Peggy is going to give him some of her homemade lemonade. This is all just exactly how it should be.

He follows Peggy into the house.

'Barry!' she calls out as they enter the wide low-ceilinged hallway. 'Your friend Juan is here!'

There's a shout from down one of the

corridors heading off from the hallway and a few seconds later, Barry bounds in, all beaming smiles and white hair and thick black-framed glasses and that handsome, domed forehead.

'Well, well, well, if it ain't Juan Abatido, my Buddhist Mexican French-Canadian gardener! I like a man who keeps to his word, Juan, and you're a man who keeps to his word.'

'Sir,' mumbles Jack, suddenly shy.

'Don't you "Sir" me you son of a bitch,' Barry snarls back in mock anger. 'Name's Barry.'

Jack smiles.

'OK Barry,' he says.

Peggy's looking at Jack coolly, cocking her head to one side as though examining him, cigarette in hand still. She's pulled off her scarf and shaken her thick auburn hair, revealing the tanned, strong face of a fifty-five-year-old. She reaches out and touches his arm.

'Here, come into the kitchen and have some of that lemonade,' she says, smiling.

An hour later, Jack's out in the garden,
digging up the second cactus Peggy wants
moved. The work's not too hard, which is good
as he's pretty out of shape and it's a fine
thing to be outside in the December sunshine
with the sun now slanting nicely in from a
clear blue sky. Once this plant is out, he'll
walk around the other side of the substantial
ranch building and dig a couple of holes the
other side to take them. Meanwhile, Barry's
in his den dealing with family business from
the department store in Phoenix which his
grandfather built and Peggy's in the lounge
looking through a pile of *Vanity Fairs*. She flips
through all the different editions until she
seems to have found what she was looking for.

'Aha!' she says out loud, with that curious
smile again. She takes the magazine and
walks over to the window where she can see
Jack digging in the garden. She looks towards
him, then down again at the open page of the

magazine, then chuckles.

'Well, who'd have thought it?' she says out loud again, quietly.

Peggy is from Muncie, Indiana. Her family were successful Midwestern industrialists who'd taken a trip down south to Phoenix in 1930 so her father could improve his health with some southern sunshine. She and her mother had frequented the big department store in Phoenix while they were there, and were served personally by the young owner, a Mr. Barry Goldwater, who patrolled the shop floor in striped trousers, a black coat and stiff white collar with a red carnation in his buttonhole. She didn't make much of the fellow but he was smitten and over the next three years, as he later said, he 'made more promises than Walter Mondale.' Every time Peggy took the train down to Phoenix with her mother and father, Barry would arrange for gifts to be taken on board at every stop the train made. When she went

around the world with her mother on a cruise,
Barry wrote to her every day. They married in
Muncie in 1934.

Peggy is smart, tough and resilient. While
Barry was away flying planes across China
during the war, she raised their four children
in Paradise Valley, taking all four on hikes
across the desert, teaching them survival
skills. She's all consideration, observation
and good common sense to Barry's breezy
instinctiveness and nose for trouble. They've
been a good partnership these last thirty
years: when Barry stuck his neck out insisting
on treating all colors the same wherever he
operated in Phoenix, she backed him up all the
way. When his Democratic political opponents
in the Presidential election he just lost
slandered him as a southern racist, her blood
boiled. But when he opens his mouth just too
quick and too wide, she's not slow to give him a
hefty kick in the shins.

She wonders which way this latest
development is going to end up. She's well aware
quite how tough a character her husband is, but
she knows how much he's gone through this last
year and she's keeping an eye on him.

An hour later, Peggy wanders out into the
garden again. Jack's round the other side
of the house now, bedding in the two cacti
into their new position. He's got them in and
he's sitting on the sandy earth, looking over
towards Camelback Mountain. His shirt is
soaked with sweat.

'Oh Juan, that's just fine!' Peggy calls out, as
she approaches. 'You've done a fine job.'

She notes how exhausted he looks already,
and how untidy the earth around the new
planting is. This isn't a gardener at all.

Jack shuffles to his feet awkwardly.

'Now,' she continues, 'you look like a man
who could do with a salami and mustard
sandwich, am I right?'

Jack musters a half smile and an embarrassed shrug.

'Well, just you rest out here in this sunshine for ten minutes and I'll call you in soon to have some lunch with us.'

With that, Peggy goes back into the house in search of Barry. He's still in his den working on family business. He looks up when she comes in.

'God damn it, Peggy,' he says. 'Just read through this quarter's accounts. Do you know how much that damn fool brother of mine is paying for coffee beans for the store? Twenty seven dollars a sack, that's what. Should be no more than twenty. I know a guy —'

She puts up her hand.

'Stop right there, Barry Goldwater,' she says. 'Just because you're out of politics doesn't mean you're going to stick your nose into running the store again. It's run perfectly well without you for at least ten years and I'm sure

Bob knows exactly what he's doing.'

'But —'

'But nothing. I'm making a sandwich for Juan, he's moved the cacti and he looks like he could do with some food inside him. Come into the kitchen in ten minutes.'

She leaves him muttering over his paperwork. She's not going to tell either of these men what she's worked out so quickly, she's going to let them sort themselves out. She's got an idea on that front too.

Soon, the three of them are sitting at one end of the carved maple dining table set off to one side of the big, open-plan kitchen. Jack's ripping eagerly through his rye bread and salami sandwich, and he's already gulped down half the glass of chilled milk Peggy put in front of him. He's not aware quite how grubby and beaten up he looks in this setting and with these people and in fact he's enjoying being Juan Abatido more as every hour passes.

'Peggy says you've done a great job already, Juan,' says Barry, taking a bite of his own sandwich. 'Don't go too fast, you'll get the damned Labor Federation on my case.'

Jack grins.

'I'm not a Labor man, Barry. I just dig the earth.'

'That's what I like to hear. You know, when my grandfather and my grandmother came from Russia in the last century and ended up here in the south west, they dug the earth to build their first house themselves. They constructed their first store with their bare hands. How —'

At this point, Peggy can't help herself, and she finishes her husband's sentence for him:

'How they did that without the help of the Federal Government I'll never know,' she says, in time with Barry, and he puts on a mock look of indignation while she laughs affectionately.

'Don't worry, Juan,' she says, 'I've lived with

49

this man for thirty years, I know every line.'

'Humph,' says Barry, carrying on eating.
'Anyway, how long you been living here in the
Valley, Juan? You here for good, or will you go
back someday?'

'To Mexico City?' Jack asks. 'Nah, I like it
here. I like it good. I been here five years now.'

'Well, good on you, Juan. I like to hear that.
You may know that I've been pretty vocal on
the topic of Mexican workers in our State.
Unlike some of my contemporaries here in the
Phoenix business community, I happen to think
that the Mexican should be as welcome as any
other person to come and make a living here.
That's the American way, always has been.
But my view hasn't changed on one thing: if
a man wants to work, let me pay him what
I think he's worth, not what some damned
union official a couple of thousand miles away
thinks he should get. If a man doesn't want
to work for me, he's perfectly free to take his

labor someplace else. I don't care if he's white,
brown, black, yellow or bright orange, I'll have
any man working for me who wants to do a
good job. Say, what do they pay you over at the
Methodist chapel?'

Jack looks uncomfortable.

'For gardening?' he asks.

'Well, yes,' says Barry. 'Unless you do some
preaching for 'em too?'

'Er, I forget,' says Jack, taking another swig
of milk.

'I'd guess it's around ten dollars a day, isn't
it Juan?' Peggy intercedes smoothly.

Jack nods his head.

'Yeah, that's right. Ten dollars a day.'

'Well, I'm strictly an Episcopalian Jew rather
than a Methodist, but I'll match those fellows,
Juan,' says Barry, putting down his sandwich.
'Ten dollars a day it is.' He extends his hand
across the table, and Jack shakes it.

'Now that you men have sorted your

business out, can I tell you what I want done next?' Peggy asks.

'Uh oh, Juan,' says Barry, winking at Jack.

'Now that Juan has moved those two cacti from the front, and a very nice job he's made of it too, we're going to turn that dinky spot into a sandpit for little Carolyn to play in this Christmas. Now, according to my diary —'

'The official diary, that's what it's called here, Juan,' says Barry, grinning and eating.

'That's as may be,' Peggy continues, unruffled, 'but by my understanding, Sir is busy on matters relating to the Grand Old Party for the rest of today but tomorrow he has a day of relaxation. So I'm proposing to show Juan where the pit is to be after lunch, he can do a little light digging to make the space right, then tomorrow you can both go and find me some of that nice pure Sonora sand.' She touches Barry's hand, smiles. 'Do you remember, dear, we used to take the children hiking over in

the White Tank mountains and the sand in the
foothills, why there's no finer. Joanne herself
used to play in that when she was Carolyn's
age. That's what we need.' She turns back to
Jack. 'What do you say to that, Juan?'

Jack grins.

'That sounds just fine, ma'am,' he says.

She turns her face to Barry, eyebrows raised.

'Your wish, my dear, is mine to be obeyed,'
he says. 'Tell you what, Juan, I'll come and
pick you up from your house then we can drive
straight over from there. Only a short drive.
Be good to catch a bit of the mountains, too; I'll
bring my camera. I'll be at yours at ten.'

That afternoon, Jack spends three hours
scratching away at the loose soil in front of
Be-Nun-I-Kin to make a circular area about ten
feet across which will take the sand. It's not
tough work and he's taking it slow. When she
sat out with him for a while to show him the
dimensions she wanted, Peggy was careful to

tell him that he could take three hours over
it and then call it a day. She can see this is
a man unused to physical labor and she can
tell, having straightened up the garden the
other side where he'd roughly inserted the
cacti to their new position, that he has little or
no experience of gardening. At one point, she
comes out with a fresh glass of lemonade and
finds him sitting cross-legged in the pit he's
made, hands clasped in prayer in front of his
chest, muttering some chant.

'I'll just leave this here, Juan,' she says
quietly.

He turns his head.

'No, you go right ahead and do your praying,
that's a sign this sandpit is going to be a happy
place.' She smiles and heads back into the
kitchen.

Later in the day, as the light begins to fade,
Jack comes down from his headstand outside
the adobe hut, opens the whiskey bottle and

sits drinking it with his back against the wall,
watching a screech owl glide low over the
sandy mountain floor.

****

Just before ten the following morning, Barry
pulls up outside Jack's hut, scattering sand
and pebbles as the car swings to a halt. He
beeps the horn. After a couple of seconds, Jack
appears in the doorway, nods, turns back inside
to pick something up, then leaves the front
door closed behind him as he heads over to the
passenger side.

'Top of the morning, Juan!' beams Barry,
pressing the ignition. 'Get in, fellow, we've got
sand to dig.'

Jack drops his leather bag onto the floor and
settles into the seat as Barry heads back down
the mountain. Before long, they've rounded
Mummy Mountain and are up heading west on

West Olive Road and Barry is in full flow.

'Boy oh boy, Juan, I just think there are
so many lessons we get in life, we never stop
learning, don't you think? Take me for example:
if I'd won that damn election, I'd be up in
Washington right now, arguing about this and
negotiating about that, making little side deals
here, little compromises there, trying to stay
true to the kind of vision we had. And don't get
me wrong, I'd have been proud to do it, proud
to have a chance of stopping the decline of this
country of ours. I don't say this as any kind of
boast, but America needed me a lot more than
it deserved Mr. Johnson and now we're in for
a hell of a time, no question. A hell of a time.
But I didn't win, Juan, and now I'm sitting here
in a car with my French-Canadian-Mexican-
Buddhist-gardener and the sun is shining and
we're heading to the desert for the day and I am
happy to say that I feel very fine about it. Very
fine indeed. Say, you feeling OK?'

All the color has drained from Jack's face.

'Could you pull over, Barry?' he mumbles. Barry eases the car off the road onto the dirt, Jack stumbles out and throws up. He stays hunkered down for a few seconds, his hands on his thighs, his head drooping. Then he straightens up, wipes his mouth on his sleeve, gets back in the car.

'Sorry,' he says. 'Ate bad food.'

Barry frowns.

'You OK to do this trip, Juan? You look like shit, fella.'

Jack nods. 'Sure,' he says. 'I'll be fine. Just some damn thing.'

'All right then,' Barry says, steering back onto the highway. 'We'll stop and get you some coffee at the gas station near the air base, settle that stomach of yours.'

They drive in silence for a while, the residential avenues of west Phoenix picked out squarely in the early morning December sunshine, the low, wide residences absorbing the fresh light. Gradually, the houses become fewer and farther between and then up ahead on the right there's a Shell sign.

'Here we go, Juan,' Barry grins. 'This is where I get my second breakfast when I'm on duty at Luke.' Barry is still an Air Reserve Major General and spends a day a month at Luke Air Force Base. There's a diner off to one side of the gas station and he pulls the car up outside.

'Good morning, Mr. Goldwater!' the young woman behind the counter calls out as they walk in. She has a red scarf tied over her blonde hair, she's maybe twenty years old, slim beneath the chequered apron. There's only a couple of tables occupied and the steam from the coffee is misting the windows. They take stools at the counter.

'Good morning, Sylvia,' says Barry. 'You're looking beautiful as ever. My friend here needs some sustenance, so we'll take your eggs and bread and as much coffee as you can pour.'

She smiles.

'Right away, Mr. Goldwater.' She looks at Jack. 'Sunny side up as well, sir?'

'Sure, thank you,' Jack mumbles.

Sylvia looks at Jack for a little longer than she needs to, then heads back into the kitchen with the order.

'This'll fix you up, Juan,' Barry whispers. 'Lord, how I love breakfast when it's served by a pretty girl.'

Jack grins weakly at him. He looks around the diner. He used to stop at places like this many times in the old days but in recent years he's gotten used to Mémère's cooking at home. There's a couple of guys, look like truckdrivers, chowing down over in a corner table and an elderly black man patiently writing in pencil in a notebook the other side of the room, a coffee beside him. Jack observes him for a while.

'They used to have a sign over the door

here, Juan,' Barry says. *'No Negroes. No Mexicans. No Indians.* I tore the damn thing down myself ten years ago. I won't live amongst that kind of thing. The Good Lord put us all on this earth to make our contribution in our own way.'

Jack looks at him.

'Are you a religious man, Barry?' he asks.

'Me? Well, I'm not given to spending much time on the matter, if you want to know. I think if a man acts according to his conscience, follows some kind of ethics, then he's a religious man I suppose. Doesn't have a lot to do with how often he gets inside a church.'

Jack nods.

'I hear you.'

Over at the door to the kitchen, Sylvia is standing with an older woman, and they're both looking over at the two men sitting at the counter. Sylvia's eyes are wide and excited. She's clutching the other woman's sleeve.

'Buddhism's like that too,' Jack continues, looking down into his coffee. 'I don't think of it as a religion. It's more a way of life. How you go about yourself. How you live.'

'Do you live well, Juan?'

'No. I do not.'

Sylvia interrupts them.

'Eggs, sunny side up, buttered bread, gentlemen,' she smiles, handing plates over the counter. 'Can I refill you, sir?' she asks Jack. She's got a really intense stare as she looks into Jack's face.

'Thank you, ma'am,' he says.

They eat in companionable silence, both of them smear the egg yolk from the plate with the bread as they finish. Now Sylvia can't hold back. She's snuck out of the counter area and is standing beside Jack. She's holding a book: *On The Road*. It's been well read, the pages are all furred up on the edge.

'Excuse me, Mister Kerouac,' she says.

'Would you please sign my copy? I've read it
three times. I can't —'

She's so flustered now she runs out of things
to say. Her pale cheeks are flushed and she's
pushing Jack's plate away with the book. Barry
looks on, intrigued. Jack drops his head.

'It means so much to me, Mister Kerouac,'
she starts again, almost breathless with nerves.
'Everything in it. I want to go to those jazz clubs,
I want to see the country from a train wagon. I
want to meet Sal Paradise and Dean Moriarty.
I'm saving up for a bus ticket to New York. I —'

Jack looks down at the book. It's the
paperback with the cover he hates, showing
sketched illustrations of debauchery and a
thoughtful young man standing in the centre
wearing a seaman's smock, looking into the
distance. The blurb bottom left says: *This is
the bible of the "Beat Generation" — the explosive
bestseller that tells all about today's wild youth and
their frenetic search for Experience and Sensation.*

There's an awkward silence. The elder
woman is standing in the doorway to the
kitchen, and the chef, a plump middle-aged
man, is standing beside her. The two truckers
have finished eating and they're looking over
towards the scene at the counter. The elderly
black man has stopped writing in his notebook
and is gazing up.

'I think you may have made a mistake,
young lady,' Barry says, smiling. 'This —'

'It's OK, Barry,' Jack interrupts him. He
takes hold of the book, then he looks up at
Sylvia. 'I'll sign it for you, ma'am,' he says,
'as long as you promise me you won't leave
Arizona and you'll stay here and you'll make a
happy life.'

She giggles nervously, pulls a pen from her
breast pocket, hands it to him.

'I can't do that,' she says, brave now. 'My
life changed when I read your book, Mister
Kerouac. That's just how it is. I'm going on the

road. I'm going in Spring.'

He's shaking his head now as he opens the book to find the title page.

'What's your name?'

'Sylvia,' she says, urgently. He writes in the book: *To Sylvia. Everything is holy Don't leave Phoenix. From someone who knows. Jack Kerouac.*

He hands it to her.

'I'll come back in the Spring,' he says, wearily. 'I hope you'll be here.'

She clutches the book to her chest, shakes her head.

'No Mister Kerouac, you won't find me here. Maybe you'll find me in New York some place. I'm going to be a writer.'

It's as though this final outburst has exhausted her. She stands for a moment, looking bewildered, then she walks swiftly back around the counter and disappears into the kitchen. Barry is looking at Jack inquisitively.

'Would you like to —,' he begins, but Jack

puts his hand up.

'Can we move on, Barry?' he asks. 'We've got Mrs. Goldwater's sand to fetch.'

Barry eyes him.

'Sure,' he says. He puts a couple of dollars down on the counter. 'Let's get going.'

Barry starts the Buick up and is skittering back onto the road before Jack's had a chance fully to close the passenger door. Barry's jaw is clenched and he stares straight ahead, not glancing to the left as they pass the air base. The peaks of White Tank Mountains are ahead of them.

'Me mentiste, Juan?' Barry says, still looking forwards.

Jack doesn't say anything.

'Dije, eres un maldito mentiroso?'

'I don't understand Spanish, Barry,' Jack says eventually.

'Well I do. I speak it pretty damn well. I speak it well because I love Mexico and

I appreciate the contribution our Spanish neighbours have made and continue to make to our culture and our society. And I would have thought that a goddamned Mexican gardener, even a Buddhist Mexican gardener with a French Canadian mother, would speak Spanish better than me. And yet you don't.'

Jack sighs. 'OK, I'm not Mexican and my name's not Juan Abatido. But at the same time, I am and it is. What did you say anyway?'

Barry turns to look at him for the first time. His face is mean.

'What did I say? I asked you if you were a goddamned liar.'

Jack shrugs. 'I'm a writer. All writers are goddamned liars.'

Barry swings the car off the road and bounces it to a halt. He yanks his door open, gets out and strides away from the car. After ten steps, he stops, turns and yells:

'Come on, fella. Out here and talk.'

Slowly, Jack heaves himself out of the front seat, walks to the front of the car and sits heavily on the bonnet. He looks down. Barry approaches, eyes screwed up behind those thick glasses as he looks into the morning sun, and he waves an arm at Jack.

'I don't know who you are, but I invited you into my home and I introduced you to my wife and she gave you some of her homemade lemonade and I want some answers, sir, right now.'

Jack looks up. His face is groggy, fleshy. His jowls hang loose. He sweeps a hand through his hair.

'My name is Jack Kerouac. The girl recognised me. I wrote that book and I wrote a few other books. You're a busy man, you don't have time to spend on this crap. But I get recognised all the time these days, which is why I thought if I came to Arizona I'd be able to get on and work and not get disrupted like I do everywhere. Only it turns out I had no work in me and I got recognised anyway and now I've treated you and your wife dishonourably and for that I apologise.'

'Kerouac, huh? I may have heard that name. Can't pretend I know any more than that. So let's get this straight: this whole Mexican thing is a pile of horseshit?'

'Well, I've spent some time there, Barry. I've spent plenty of time there. I thought I might move there but there's no way I could persuade Mémère.'

'Who's Mémère?'

'She's my mother. She's waiting for me back in Florida.'

'You told me she was dead, you son of a bitch. Who lies about something like that?'

Jack shrugs. 'I told you Barry, writers —'

'Writers lie, yeah, yeah, you said that. Well let me tell you, sir, I think that stinks. Don't you think what a man says has any import, any consequence? Do you think a man can just say whatever the hell he likes and damn the consequences? What do you think I've spent the last thirty years of my life doing if not trying to speak honestly and truthfully? What kind of a world do we live in if a man can pretend his own mother is dead?'

Barry shakes his head, walks off a little. Then he comes back, shaking his hand once more.

'You want to know how old my mother is? She's eighty nine years old. She lives in Phoenix and I've got a good mind to take you to her right now and make you apologise to her on behalf of — what did you call her?'

'Mémère,' Jack says.

'That's right,' Barry replies. 'So the French Canadian stuff, that's true?'

Jack nods. 'My parents both. Dad's long gone. I promised him on his deathbed I'd look after Mémère and that's what I try and do. She's a good woman, Barry. She wouldn't take

offence at my foolishness. I understand I have
offended you but I look after my ma.'

Barry looks at him, nods thoughtfully.
They're both quiet. A truck drives past them
throwing up some sand, making the car shudder
in its slipstream. Jack screws his eyes tight.

'OK,' Barry says after a while. 'Maybe I
dived in there a little. Peggy says I need to
watch that. But this is my state, fellow: I don't
like people to lie to me, and I particularly don't
like them to lie to me in my own state. And now
there's that young girl involved and I'll have
to talk to her father at some point if you've
put some damn fool ideas into her head.' He
walks around in slow circles, stroking his chin.
'However,' he continues, 'you've been gracious
in your apology. Tell me your name again.'

'Jack Kerouac.'

'OK, Jack. And what was the name of that
book that so turned the head of young Sylvia
just now?'

'*On The Road*. Came out seven years ago.'

'Must have sold well to find its way down to Paradise Valley?'

'I guess.'

'You don't seem very pleased about it.'

'Oh, I'm pleased enough with the book. It's not what I want to be known for, though.'

'What do you want to be known for?'

'Right now? Nothing at all, Barry. Nothing at all. Nada.'

'Pah. Now you're lying again. No man writes a book that sells enough copies for some kid in a diner in Phoenix to go weak at the knees when she meets the author — no man who writes a book like that doesn't want to be admired.'

'OK, you're right. What do I want? I want for my books, my writing, to be understood the way I wrote it. I want people to read the prose and understand that this is a new way to write that is more honest, that this is all a part of what is great about the American

soul. I want people to read my words and hear
Charlie Parker. I don't want kids like that girl
to read my work like it's some kind of damn
life manual. Who the heck wants to spend their
nights and days standing by the road with their
thumb out, sleeping in dive joints and drinking
port wine because you can't afford anything
else? That's all bullshit. I just happened to do
that because I'm too dumb to make any money
and I had to spread myself across this country
somehow if I was going to find Walt Whitman
and that was the only way I knew how. But I
did it so I could write the words, Barry. That's
all it was about: the words. And no one wants
to talk about the words. They want to talk
about goddamn foolish nonsense, they want to
make me into some kind of dancing bear, they
want to put my name on T-shirts so they can
sell 'em to that kid in the diner. And I don't
want nothing of any of that. I'd rather sit up
there on the mountain and drink whiskey and

fly with the eagles.'

Barry eyes him now.

'Well, at least you're talking like a man now,' he says, finally. Jack's still slumped on the bonnet of the car. Barry rubs his chin again. 'How many copies you sell of that book, anyway?'

Jack looks up once more, weary as hell.

'*On The Road*? I think about a million so far. I got to ask Sterling about the numbers, I got some bills to pay at home.'

'A million, huh? I put out my book, *Conscience*, in '60 and it's sold two million. But I don't get Sylvia coming up to me with that doe-eyed look and telling me it's changed her life.'

'Then you're a lucky man, Barry Goldwater,' Jack says. 'I didn't read your book.'

'And I didn't read yours, so that makes us square.'

For the first time, Jack grins. When he

smiles, you finally see the Jack that's lying
underneath all that exhaustion.

'What say we go find Mrs. Goldwater's
sand?' Jack says, pushing himself up from
the car metal. 'You're paying Juan Abatido
ten bucks for today's job. You're wasting your
money right here.'

Barry laughs.

'OK, hotshot. But boy, I tell you, you'd better
put your back into it. I want to see that shovel
work.'

****

Barry had parked the car in the foothills of
the White Tank mountains, tucked in between
two towering Saguaro cacti that stood twenty
or more feet over the Buick. There was no one
else around that December morning, the sky
was blue and the sun was beginning to heat the
desert floor. The two men had spent an hour

patiently filling up several old hessian sacks
with the fine sand that Peggy had specified she
wanted. The ground all about was hard and
covered with a thin layer of Sonora sand which
glinted like crystal in the morning light. They
didn't talk much, focusing instead on the task,
helping each other out: one holding the sack
open, the other scooping in the sand which he'd
scraped into a pile. Once each sack was filled,
they'd take an end each and jigger over to the
open boot of the car and swing it in.

Once they'd filled five sacks, and the rear of
the car was sitting a little lower than before,
Barry stood back, hands on his hips, nodding
approvingly.

'Well Jack, we did OK, I'd say,' he says and
puts out a hand. Jack takes it and they shake.
They've both got sweat on their brows now.

'Mrs. Goldwater's going to be happy, Barry.'

'And that, young fella, is always a good
thing. Now, what time is it?' He looks at his

watch, an old Rolex chronometer that used to belong to his father. 'Midday. Why don't we take a short hike up into the hills? It's a beautiful day and you happen to be in the company of a man who knows these trails extremely well. You got some powder in your horn still?'

'Yes I do, sir.'

'Well then.'

Barry slams the boot shut, reaches into the rear seat of the Buick to grab his camera, and they head off in the direction of the peaks.

'On journeys through the States we start,' says Jack.

'What's that?'

'Walt Whitman.'

'Poetry, huh? I never took to it.'

They walk in silence for a while. Before long, the ground begins to ascend and Barry motions that they'll take the right fork where the bare outline of the path splits. There

are scattered boulders on either side, scrub
bushes with green leaves and here and there
the Saguaro standing like sentinels.

'Know where those sacks came from, Jack?'
Barry asks after a while.

Jack looks up, momentarily brought out of
the daydream he'd been having.

'Tell me.'

'I've had an interest for years now in a
trading post up north at the foot of the Navajo
Mountain. Up close to Rainbow Bridge, you
know it? Beautiful country. It was a trading
point for most of the last century and about
twenty years ago, a few fellows and I, we
acquired the trading post and built a lodge
next to it so's people could stay and make their
trek to the Bridge. Up until some damn cowboy
burned the lodge down in '51 with his cigarette,
we were doing good money up there. Remember
once, I sold some bales of hay to an old Navajo
woman and when I tried to help her pitch 'em

up onto the roof of her cart, she punched me
in the jaw.' He laughs out loud. 'Tough people,
the Navajo. Good people. Anyway, those hessian
sacks were all I salvaged from the fire. Been
meaning to find a use for 'em for ten years or
more now.'

'What territory is this?' Jack asked.

'White Tank? This is Hohokam land. They
farmed this land for over a thousand years.
They were smart, they worked out how to
preserve water. There are still canals working in
Phoenix which they built hundreds of years ago.'

'They still own this land?'

Barry turns to him with an amused frown.

'Don't be a damn fool. You know as well
as I do this is United States territory. But the
Hohokam weren't a tribe like the Hopi or the
Navajo, they kind of dispersed into other clans
a few hundred years ago. But I see it as our
duty to preserve their memory. We're making
this whole mountain range —' he sweeps an

arm all around him — 'into a national park, opens next year.'

'Good thing we took the sand now, then,' says Jack, and Barry chuckles.

'I'd like to see you try and tell Mrs. Goldwater what she can and can't do,' he says.

The path steepens now and they climb one behind the other for a little while until Barry, up ahead of Jack who's now feeling this climb in his legs, stops and calls back:

'Keep going, boy! Come take a look at this!'

Jack joins him soon, breathing heavily. They're now about halfway up the mountain and while he catches his breath, Jack turns back to look the way they've come. Out in the distance, the chequerboard roads of Phoenix lie neatly in the winter sunshine, the rolling hills of Mummy and Camelback mountains far away marking the edges of Paradise Valley. After a moment's rest, he turns. Barry is standing by a rock, grinning.

'Gardener, my ass,' he says. 'How you got to fool me you were Mexican *and* a gardener I'll never know. Anyway, take a look.'

He points at several symbols painted onto the rock. One looks like a snake, another rounder, like the sun maybe. They're ancient, fading somewhat now but with the color pigment strong enough to be clearly visible.

'Petroglyphs,' Barry says. 'Maybe Hohokam, maybe even from before then. At least 1500 years old.'

'Wow.'

'Imagine that, Mister Writer. Two fellows like you and me, 1500 years ago, on this same mountain, sticking down these messages so's their friends would know which way to go, probably to find water. Further up, there's what we call the Tanks, natural basins formed in the granite where water can be found even in summer. I was going to show you them but —'

'I know, I know,' Jack says, sitting down. 'I'm

beat, I'll admit it.'

Barry, of course, doesn't catch the unintended irony. He sits down next to Jack and they both look back out east across the plain.

'How do you know those symbols are telling people where to find water?' Jack asks after a while.

Barry shrugs. 'Just a guess. No one really knows. But why else would you draw on the rocks?'

'Plenty of reasons, maybe,' says Jack, turning his head to look once more at the petroglyphs. 'Take a look at the snake: that could mean plenty. The Indians, you know they talk about the snake like he's the symbol of our life force, he's the energy that coils up inside us, shoots up through us like a mad exploding volcano of pure life and bursts up out into the world, all joy and beauty. That's what the snake is to the Indians, the Indians out in

India, I mean. And I read that our American Indians, they came across from India into the Northwest when there was no sea between Alaska and the Russians. So, you know, I'm just saying, maybe the Hohokam's ancestors brought that knowledge over to America and maybe that's what they were drawing. The snake of life. The stuff that makes us human.'

'I couldn't say. But if I was stuck up here, I'd be grateful if the fellow who'd travelled before me had pointed out where the water was.'

Jack nods. 'True enough.'

They sit in companionable silence for a while. A buzzard circles lazily above them in the blue December sky. Barry picks up a stone and throws it down the steep slope, watching it clatter into a gully. He wipes the dust from his hands on his denim jeans. Jack's dreaming again now, dreaming about tribes migrating across the Siberian tundra, forging their way into the land that is now Alaska, bringing their

spirits and their songs and their Gods down
into the warmer and warmer southern lands,
finding these mountains, kneeling down beside
the rock with pigments ready to —

'So tell me, Jack — I ain't calling you Juan
any more, though I confess I liked the fellow —
tell me what got young Sylvia so hot under the
collar about that book of yours.'

Jack looks startled. *On The Road?* Oh Jeez, I
don't know, Barry.'

'Come on, try harder. What was she so
wrapped up in with all that talk of jazz clubs
in New York and sitting on train wagons and
who's that guy she mentioned, Sal Paradise?
He from round here?'

'Oh.' That's the first time Jack's realised the
link. Sal Paradise, his fictionalised self in *On The
Road*. That's the first time in four weeks he's
caught the link. 'That's funny, I guess,' he says,
not smiling. 'No, Sal's not from round here.'

He's staying in Paradise Valley. And he's

living on Mummy Mountain. Good grief. Jack
feels a wave of nausea sweeping over him now,
and he closes his eyes to the swaying view
of the scenery below. Sal Paradise. Christ, he
hates that book. He can hear Barry saying
something but he doesn't know what it is. He's
sweating in the cold December sun.

'— so come on,' he finally hears Barry
saying. 'Tell me the story.'

Jack opens his eyes and Barry's there,
always smiling, and it's a fine American smile
and there's no malice in it and this is all of
Jack's making, all of it, all of it. He's got to pull
himself together.

'The book? That book?'

Barry nods encouragingly.

'It's...' Jack falters again. He's trying to
grasp at something, something about Neal
Cassady turning up in New York in that winter
of 1946, about how Neal stood there naked
at the doorway in that apartment in Spanish

84

Harlem and how his life changed and how
he and Neal spent the next ten years trying
to embrace the whole of America with their
outspread arms and their innocence and
holiness but it won't come out, and he finds
himself saying,

'I don't know, Barry. It's about my brother
Gerard dying up in Lowell when I was four
years old, I guess. He died and there was
nothing I could do about it and nothing was
good after that. My Dad, Leo, died and he loved
this country but it never loved him back and
my sister's gone now too and it's just me and
Mémère and she's waiting for me to come home
for Christmas.'

Jack's head drops down and he stops talking.
The cold air is silent and the gold December
sun is still and implacable. Barry takes a stick
and draws some lines in the gravel of the
mountainside. Then he shakes his shoulders,
sniffs the air and looks up at Jack.

'Say, how was your war?' Barry asks.

'My war?' Jack looks up, confused.

'Yeah, where did you serve?'

'Oh. The Navy. Only I got invalided out.' He points down at his legs. 'Got this damn phlebitis, you know. Sports injury at High School. Knocked me out of football, then knocked me out of the war.'

Jack's still wily enough not to reveal to the war hero Barry Goldwater that he got dishonourably discharged after eight days in the Navy for 'indifferent character.'

'Too bad,' says Barry. 'Well, we all did our duty, that's for sure. Football, that's a northern man's game. Down here, we ride horses.'

'Ridden a freight train, Barry, never a horse.'

'And that's what young Sylvia wants to do now, after reading your book? She wants to ride a freight train? That how you got to Phoenix, or you stick your thumb out?'

'Neither. I flew from Tampa drinking

Highballs,' says Jack, and they both laugh.

'Well, plenty of fellows who came back from the war, they had to hitchhike and ride freight trains to find work, I understand that,' Barry continues. 'Same thing happened in the '30s: when the economy's down a man needs to use every opportunity he can to find work. But listen here, Jack: you sound like you're pushing this bum life. Is that what's got Sylvia excited? Sleeping on the side of the road and panhandling for cents? You're confusing me. That doesn't sound like the kind of future we should be offering our kids. Look at you — you just told me you took a nice comfortable seat on an aeroplane. Why not encourage young Sylvia to make her way in life so she can sit and watch the world go by and drink Highballs like you? What's the point of putting ideas into her head about heading off to New York to be a writer?'

Jack shakes his head.

'That's not what I'm trying to do, Barry,'

he sighs. 'I'm not trying to offer any future to anyone. I never wanted anyone to do what I did. I just wanted to set words down on a page and if you want to set the words down right, you got to spend your whole life doing it and not think about anything else.'

'Hmm,' says Barry, frowning. 'Well, maybe I just don't have the book man's perspective. I sure would like to talk to young Sylvia and undo that spell you put on her. Her father's a good man, got a hardware store over in Glendale. He helped run my campaign here in Arizona, much good though it did us all. I'll go talk to them.' He glances at Jack. 'And don't look so bleak, I won't make you come with me. We're all born free on this earth, Jack, and our duty is to help each other to retain that freedom in the face of government interference, foreign aggression and damn nonsense dressed up in fancy books.'

Jack laughs. 'First time anyone's called my

writing fancy, Barry.'

Barry nods. 'Boy, there's a first time for everything.' He slaps Jack on the back. 'Now, what we're going to do is take Mrs. Goldwater's sand to her, you're going to finish that job I'm paying you so damn much for, then we're going to have a drink. But first, I'm going to take your picture. While you were sitting there thinking your writer thoughts, I was working out the shot.'

Barry starts to take the cover off his camera. Jack shakes his head.

'I don't know, Barry. I don't really like having my photo taken.'

'It's OK. The shot I have in mind is of that peak up there.' He points to the summit. 'You're kind of incidental. But I need a human figure in it for perspective. Doesn't matter if your back's turned. You wait here, I've got to head down to that rock down there to take the picture.'

****

Many years later, Barry's daughter Joanne
was sorting through her father's photograph
collection, trying to help the Phoenix museum
put together a retrospective of his famous
black and white portraits of Arizona. In his
study at Be-Nun-I-Kin there were piles and
piles of the work he'd painstakingly processed
himself in his own makeshift darkroom and
she spent days going through them one by
one, smiling here and there as she recognised
a landmark from one of the many hiking trips
her father had taken her and her siblings
on such a long time ago. As she was sorting through them, placing them into different piles, she came upon a photograph she
couldn't remember seeing before. There was
something melancholy about this one: it was
one of the mesa portraits, the striking hill
formations dotted all around the outskirts

of Phoenix, and this one was dominated by
a peak — maybe White Tank, she thought?
But what made it so melancholy was that
her father, never a melancholy man in any
way, had somehow framed the peak so that a
human figure could be made out in the fore-
ground, very small because of the distance
perspective, and with its back turned so that
all you could see was a slouched male figure,
the back of the head tilted making you understand that he was looking up towards the top
of the hill. The figure looked almost fragile
in its lonely insignificance against the brute
textures of the granite mountain.

'No, not that one,' she said aloud to herself.
'Dad wouldn't have liked that one. Too sad.'

****

It's late afternoon and Barry's keeping up a
running commentary over his shoulder to Peggy

as he and Jack stagger to and from the open
trunk of the Buick with the filled hessian sacks.

'Took young Juan here for a stroll up to the
tanks, darling,' he calls out, a big grin on his
face as they tip another pile of Sonora sand
into the pit. 'You should have seen him. Fit
young gardener like him, I had to let him sit
down and rest.'

Peggy is eyeing them both with an amused
glint in her eye.

'Not everyone is quite as magnificent as you,
dear,' she says.

'Funny though,' Barry continues, giving Jack
a hefty slap on the back as they stand back
to admire the pit, 'you'd think a young fellow,
Mexican at that, who spent his day on physical
work, you'd think he'd be a bit fitter 'n that,
wouldn't you?'

Jack won't take the bait, trudges back
towards the car to fetch another sack. Barry
can't help chuckling as he follows him.

'You do seem to have enjoyed your day out,' Peggy continues. She takes a cigarette out of the pocket in her apron. 'Anyone would think you had a story to tell.'

Barry looks back at her as she lights her cigarette.

'Oh I do, I do,' he calls out. 'Don't I, Juan? Got to finish the job first, though, don't we?'

The two men reach into the trunk and haul out the last sack of sand. They drag it across the rocky ground and with one last heave, empty it into the pit. Barry strides over to the fence and grabs hold of a rake that's leaning against it.

'Here,' he says, still grinning as he passes it to Jack. 'You're the gardener, Juan. Why don't you make the surface of that sandpit nice and dandy?'

Jack shakes his head ruefully but there's the trace of a smile on his lips. He takes the rake and, slowly and carefully, levels the surface of the sand. The crystals of the white sand glint in the late afternoon sun and there is silence now, just the gentle sound of the rake being dragged across as Jack focuses all his attention on the job at hand and Barry stands back, hands on hips and broad smile on face, while Peggy smokes and watches. Finally, Jack straightens up, takes one more look at the neat sandpit with the raked lines drawn across its surface, then says, to no-one in particular:

'Think that should do it.'

The stillness is broken by Peggy's clapping hands.

'That is exactly how I imagined it!' she cries. 'I'm so pleased, thank you so much, Juan.'

'Now what we're going to do is celebrate this here sandpit with a drink,' says Barry, stomping off towards the house. 'Just wait there, both of you, and I shall return.'

'Very glad you're pleased, Mrs. Goldwater,' Jack mumbles. He looks a little sheepish again, now he's out here on his own with her.

'I can't tell you how pleased I am,' she says, touching the sleeve of his shirt. 'Little Carolyn is simply going to adore it. Now all we have to do is get some Christmas lights out here in the garden and it'll be all ready for her.'

There's a bang as the kitchen door shuts behind him and Barry strides back across the yard clutching a bottle of Old Crow and three glasses.

'Now,' he says, passing the glasses out, 'I suggest that we make a toast. What shall it be, my friend?' he asks Jack, pouring a healthy shot of bourbon into Jack's glass, then Peggy's, although she places a warning hand over it to limit the amount.

'Well,' Jack says, eyeing the sandpit once more, 'how about we send a prayer to the holy white shining moonspirit to watch over this pit and keep it pure and ecstatic.'

Barry frowns as he finishes slopping Old

Crow into his glass but Peggy laughs.

'Oh yes, that's just fine!' she says and clinks her glass against both the others. 'To our pure and ecstatic sandpit.'

They take a slug of bourbon and Barry turns to his wife.

'Now then, Mrs. Goldwater,' he says. 'I have something of a surprise to reveal to you about our friend Juan, here.'

Jack's still looking into the sandpit. Most of his bourbon is gone already.

'Oh, now let me try and guess,' Peggy says. 'Don't rush your surprise. Let me try and work it out.'

Barry laughs. 'Oh, you'll never work this out, darling,' he says, winking at Jack who's still staring down at the sand.

'Well, let me just try,' Peggy says. 'You know how I like a puzzle. Now, let me think.'

Barry can hardly contain himself but he lets his wife ponder, watches her eagerly as she casts her eyes from Jack to the sandpit to her husband and back to Jack again.

'Now then,' Peggy says. 'My first thought is, that our friend Juan is maybe not quite as Mexican as he had us think at first.'

Barry looks surprised.

'Well,' he says. 'Go on.'

'My second thought is that Juan may not have spent such a great part of his working life as a gardener, either,' Peggy says, swilling the bourbon in her glass thoughtfully.

'Jeez, I told you she was good,' Barry says to Jack. 'And your third thought, Mrs. Goldwater?'

'My third thought is that Juan is not actually the name his mother gave him, although it's close.'

Now Jack can't help himself, he looks up at Peggy and grins.

'Oh, of all the mad, ridiculous things,' Peggy says, laughing, 'I never could have guessed

we'd have Mister Jack Kerouac helping us
make a sandpit for little Carolyn!'

And with that, she leans over and kisses his
cheek.

'Thank you, Jack,' she says.

'Hold on just a second,' Barry interrupts,
his big brow creased with frowns. 'How the
damndest hell did you know that this man is —'

Peggy clutches her husband's arm and
kisses his cheek too.

'Sometimes you're just too busy to see
what's in front of your face, dear,' she says.
'Jack here is a famous man.' She pulls out
her copy of *Vanity Fair* from the pocket of her
apron, and shows them both the page inside
where his photograph sits atop an article on
the Beat Generation. In the photograph, Jack
is standing on a street corner in New York, a
grin on his face and his arm resting on the
shoulder of another man. 'Why I only read this
in the summer. I knew I recognised his face the

moment he turned up.'

Barry reaches over and takes the magazine. He looks at Jack.

'*Vanity* huh? Boy oh boy, Jack, you're slippier than a damn rattlesnake.'

Jack looks at the magazine with disgust.

'I never asked to be in that damned thing, Barry. It's no better than cow shit, if you excuse me, ma'am.'

Barry laughs. 'Well, I won't argue with you on that one, no offence to the lady here.'

'Comes in useful every now and then, though, doesn't it?' Peggy smiles sweetly. 'Anyways, Jack, I'm sorry if I broke your cover, or whatever it is you're doing. You probably just wanted a bit of peace and quiet. Well, you don't often get that when my husband turns up.'

'Oh, I really don't mind, Mrs. Goldwater,' Jack says sheepishly. 'I voted for your husband and I'm damn glad to have had the chance to meet you both. It's not as though I've got any writing

done here, anyhow. I could take to this work.' He
points at the sandpit and they all laugh.

Barry reaches over and refills Jack's glass,
then his. Peggy's is still full.

'I haven't forgotten,' he says, pulling out his
wallet. 'I owe you for two days. Twenty dollars
I believe.'

Jack smiles.

'I'll take that, Barry,' he says, accepting the
money. 'I think I earned it. First honest day's
work I've done in a long time.'

'Don't know about honest,' Barry shoots back.

'That's enough of that,' says Peggy. 'You'll
stay for some supper, I hope, Jack? You two
men can sit out here and put the world to
rights while I go and make us some food.'

She walks back to the house and Barry fills
both their glasses.

'Let's just hunker down here and watch the
sun go down, my friend,' he says.

They sit down on two granite boulders

beside the sandpit. The sun is reaching low out west now and there's a little chill in the air. They can hear the gentle clatter from Peggy's cooking in the kitchen.

'Sorry about all the, you know...' Jack starts.

'Oh, phooey,' Barry says. 'Man has a right to a little peace and quiet when he wants it. I should have left you trekking down that highway. Always sticking my nose in.'

He clinks Jack's glass and they both drain them once more. He reaches for the bottle.

'So what are you going to do now, Barry?' Jack asks.

Barry looks up.

'I'm going to drink this bottle of Old Crow with you, that's what I'm going to do.'

'No, I mean, you know, in politics.'

'Oh.' Barry takes a drink. He's silent for a while. Then,

'Well, there's some years left in me, Jack. I'm too old for business, Peggy's right. Business

is a young man's game and besides, I don't
much like a lot of the so-called business
practices I see creeping in here today. I see
men making too much profit when they don't
need to. Any damn fool can take advantage of
the market, but that's not what the market's
there for. The market is what it sounds like,
it's a place where people come and exchange
things. I'll find some coffee and I'll make a
little profit on packaging it up and selling it to
you. But if there's a scarcity of coffee today,
why the hell should I charge you more than
I did yesterday? That's not right. I fear we're
becoming a nation that is more concerned with
amassing fortunes than in working alongside
our fellow man. We did OK today, didn't we?
The high-flying writer and the out-of-work
politician? We did what we set out to do, didn't
we? And now we're sitting down at the end of
the day to share our thoughts. And that's a fine
thing, in my mind.'

He clinks Jack's glass.

'No, I'll leave business to the younger
folk. If you want to know, I think my days in
Washington aren't over. Four years' time, I
may have to get back on the stump. The people
of Arizona here, they won't be served well by
this federal government. The people of America
won't be served well by this federal government.
The only question is just how much damage that
bastard Johnson can inflict on the American
people over the next four years.'

'What kind of a guy is he?'

'Johnson? If he was sat here with us now
and told us what a fine sunset it was, I'd have
to put my damn glasses on and stand up on
that rock there and check that it was true.
Jack Kennedy, he wasn't like that. Jack was
my friend. You could sit with him here now and
you'd be as fine as can be. Oh he was wrong
on just about everything, particularly on the
Soviets, and he and I fought like cats about

that, but he never lied to you. I miss that fellow very much.'

They sip their drinks.

'I never got to thinking about politics much,' Jack says after a while. 'My Dad, he hated Roosevelt, he hated all the Labor Law stuff. He thought Americans made their own beds. Only he was bitter by the end, cos his bed got pretty lean. He always wanted me to be a doctor or something.'

'He'd have been proud of your success, though, wouldn't he?'

'Success?' Jack looks into his glass. 'I never thought of it that way, Barry. It sure doesn't feel that way most of the time. But anyhow, I never liked to think about politics. Me and Mémère, we never talk about it at home. I think we're all just part of a dream, we're all just part of a tune and every so often the drummer shifts the beat.'

'I hear you. The American people don't like

politics, generally, and there's a good reason
why they don't: it's a damn crooked horse
race, is what it is. The things I've seen and the
things I've heard in Washington, why they'd
make the hair on the back of your neck stand
straight up. But my problem, Jack, is I can't
leave it alone, just like I couldn't leave you to
the peace of your thoughts on the highway the
other evening. Certain things I know to be right
and certain things to be wrong and I can't keep
my damn mouth shut.'

'It's a good thing. Country needs you.'

'Well, that's kind of you to say,' Barry
replies, filling their glasses again. 'Maybe it
does, and maybe it doesn't. But I confess, I
am fearful for this country of ours. Used to
be a time when every man took responsibility
for his life and for the lives of his family, his
friends, his neighbours. 'We, the people' —
that's what the Constitution says. Not 'We,
the government'. But there's a change afoot,

I can smell it. The man in the Union office in Baltimore telling working men what they can and can't do, the college kids who are moving into Washington with all their plans for laws and regulations and spending, the families who are paying more and more taxes and not asking why. You know what it's all doing? It's taking away our rights as free men to live as we wish, so long as we don't impinge upon the lives of our neighbours. What the hell else is there, if we're not free?'

'Maybe some folks don't want to be free, Barry. You ever consider that?'

Barry is quiet for a moment, and the air is distinctly colder now the sun has slipped below the mountains out east.

'We can't think that, Jack,' he says finally, his voice much quieter. 'We just can't. That's…' He pauses again. 'That's the end of everything.'

****

Peggy's cornbread pie soaked up some of that
Old Crow an hour later. She'd taken Barry
aside after calling them in for their supper and
while Jack was in the bathroom.

'Just go slow on that bourbon, dear. You'll
need to drive that poor man home after supper
and I don't want you —'

'I know, darling. There's a...what is it?...
there's a sadness in that fellow, I think. Struck
me today, spending time with him. I was damn
near ready to punch him this morning, but you
can't stay angry with a man who's so beaten
down already. I sure would like to see him back
on his feet.'

'Well, maybe you will. You're as soft as a
cotton field, Mister Goldwater.' She kissed him
on the cheek as Jack came back into the room.

Now the three of them are sitting around
the big kitchen table and the pie dish is almost
scraped clean. Barry is sipping on a bottle of
beer, Peggy's finishing her glass of red wine

and Jack is almost at the bottom of the bottle
of Old Crow, which stands beside his plate.
He's telling them about his time over at Big
Sur four years ago, when he stayed on his own
at Lawrence Ferlinghetti's hut down in Bixby
Canyon on the sea.

'Oh and every night I'd clamber down the
rocks from the old cabin and it was dark and
real slippery and I had my notebook and my
pencil and a torch and I got all the way down
to the big boulders on the beach where the
waves kept crashing and crishing and slapping
all onto the stone and sussifying and slipping
over the sand and I had my torch and the
wind kept trying to whip the notebook out of
my hand and I played the torch on the pages
and just sat there and wrote down what the
sea was saying and I did that every night,
sitting on that boulder and listening to what
the sea was saying and trying to write it down
just as she said it like she was whispering

these words to me that I'd never heard before and no one had ever heard before and wrote everything down and I kept writing until I was exhausted then I'd go back up to the cabin and fall asleep and the next night I'd be down there again.'

He pours the last of the whisky into his glass.

'And that's just what I'm trying to say,' he continues, looking up at Barry, his eyes filmy and his face blotched with red, 'that's what I've been trying to tell you, old Barry, that's what I've been trying to get over, the words, the words, trying to make the words be the words that they should be and not some dumbass fink crap — excuse me, ma'am — that the *New York Times* will pat you on the back and say, well done boy, that's the boy, here's a prize, you've been a good boy.'

Barry feels Peggy's shoe tapping his shin under the table.

'Well Jack,' he says, sitting back in his chair

and smiling broadly, 'that's all probably very true, but this old fellow is a bit long in the tooth for late night discussions. I think I'm going to drive you back home, my friend.'

Jack shakes his head.

'No, no, it's just what I'm trying to say to you both is...' He stops, and stares at the empty bottle beside his plate. His shoulders slump. Peggy reaches over and puts her hand on his arm.

'Jack,' she says softly, 'it's been a genuine privilege having you here in our home. You will always be a welcome visitor, any time at all.'

Barry pushes back his chair, stands up, walks around the table.

'Come on, my Mexican French Canadian Buddhist friend,' he says, smiling. 'I'm taking you back up the mountain.'

****

Three days later, Barry decides to swing by
Jack's hut on Mummy Mountain on the way
to see his own mother in Phoenix. He knocks
on the door of the hut, walks around it, calls
out Jack's name a couple of times. There's no
answer, just the echo of his own voice back
from the side of the mountain.

At about this time, Jack is disembarking
from the two-day Amtrak rail journey from
Phoenix back to Tampa, back home two weeks
ahead of his planned schedule. When he'd got
up the morning after the day at the White
Tanks, sick with alcohol and remorse, he'd
packed his bag, locked the cabin and walked
down the mountain into Phoenix. There wasn't
a flight back home for six days, so he bought
a train ticket. He spent the two long days on
the cross country rail journey getting through
the last of his rye whiskey and by the time he
reached Tampa, he barely knew who he was.
The cab driver who took him the twenty miles

over to St Petersburg and Mémère had to stop
the car twice to let him out to be sick at the
side of the road.

On Christmas Day, a couple of weeks later,
Jack and his mother pull a cracker and share a
bottle of sweet wine. Jack raises his glass in a
toast:

'Happy Christmas, Barry,' he says and
Mémère says,

'Who's Barry, Ti Jean?' and Jack smiles,
shakes his head:

'Oh nothing, ma. Happy Christmas.'

Barry and Peggy have a houseful of family
on Christmas Day, there's shouting and
laughter and Barry does dress up as Santa and
little Carolyn has to be persuaded to leave her
sandpit to come indoors to eat.

****

Five years later, Barry and Peggy are sitting
in the audience of the newly-completed International Hotel in Las Vegas. They're here,
along with some friends from Arizona, to see
the opening night of Elvis Presley's reinven-
tion of his career on stage with a live band
and orchestra. The inside of the auditorium is
huge, brilliantly illuminated, with more famous
names sitting at the luxury stageside tables
than even graced the Rat Pack's shows eight
years earlier at the Sands. Elvis is wearing
a midnight blue karate tunic designed by Bill
Belew just for this show, he's thin as a knife,
his black hair is slick and he moves like nobody
else will ever do again. He opens the show with
Blue Suede Shoes, runs straight into *I Got A
Woman*, *Jailhouse Rock*, *Don't Be Cruel*.

Barry's enjoying the show as much as
everyone else. The crowd are whooping and
hollering from the very first song and the
great and the good of American society throw

themselves into another great American reincarnation. Elvis is very much in the building.

Midway through the set, Elvis slows the pace down with a medley tribute to the Beatles. He sings *Yesterday* in that vibrato, baritone voice ('there's a shadow hanging over me') and something triggers inside of Barry. As he has done occasionally over the last five years, he remembers those two days in Paradise Valley after he picked up Jack Kerouac by the side of the road. He never saw Jack again, never got a reply to the one letter he sent enquiring after him. The melancholy sensation afflicts him, and he reaches over to squeeze Peggy's hand. She's loving the show and she smiles back at him, then turns to watch Elvis again.

As *Yesterday* ends, Elvis looks over to his drummer, Ronnie Tutt. He nods at Ronnie, who grins at him and reaches out to quieten the still-ringing cymbals, then begins a loud 4:4 beat on the bass drum as Elvis turns back to the crowd and says:

   'Here's a new one for y'all.'

   As *Suspicious Minds* begins its inevitable, rampant path to its crescendo, with Ronnie almost destroying the drum kit each time Elvis finishes singing 'Because I love you so much, baby' and the horns shriek up into the rafters and Elvis shakes his entire being to Ronnie's frenzied rolls, Barry can't think about anything other than Jack Kerouac. He's suddenly overwhelmed by an inexplicable and very unfamiliar sense of despair, relating to a man he met briefly five years before. While everyone around him is on their feet and dancing with abandon and delight, Barry stays sitting at the table, raises his glass to some unseen ghost, takes a long drink.

****

Three months later, Jack Kerouac dies in St
Anthony's hospital in St Petersburg, Florida,
from an abdominal haemorrhage. He is forty
seven years old.

ENDS

About the Author – Simon Petherick

Simon Petherick is the author of four novels — *The Last Good Man, The Damnation Of Peter Pan, English Arcadia* and *Like Fire Unbound* — as well as a number of non-fiction titles and

several filmscripts. He originally worked in London as a government writer at the UK's Central Office of Information and subsequently worked in both Europe and the Baltic States as a communications specialist. He has spent time in the United States, particularly in the southwestern states of Arizona and California. He currently lives in London.

https://simonpetherick.com
Twitter: @SimonTPetherick

Acknowledgements

Jack and Barry evolved over many years of
reading Kerouac and listening to Bob Dylan and
Elvis Presley. While still at school, I listened to
the Dylan line in *I Shall Be Free Number 10 — If
you think I'm going to let Barry Goldwater move
in next door and marry my daughter, you must
think I'm crazy* — and wondered at the time
what this Barry Goldwater could have done
to incur Dylan's irony. Decades later, I read
in the singer's first volume of autobiograhy,
Chronicles, that "my favourite politician
was Arizona Senator Barry Goldwater, who
reminded me of Tom Mix, and there wasn't
any way to explain that to anybody." So it
turned out the Sixties irony was double-edged. I
spent a long time reading up on Goldwater: the
selection of his writings made by John W Dean
and Barry M Goldwater Jr, *Pure Goldwater*;

the multi-million selling *The Conscience of a Conservative*; Rick Pearlstein's Before *The Storm*; William F. Buckley Jr.'s *Flying High*. I most enjoyed the beautiful 1967 Random House illustrated edition of Goldwater's photographs, *People And Places*, which contained typically pithy summaries of each by the author. For Paradise Valley, I enjoyed Douglas B. Sydnor's *Paradise Valley Architecture*, and I also benefited from the factual critique of my Paradise Valley friend, Vicki Ratliff. I re-read *Kerouac* by Ann Charters and *Minor Characters* by Joyce Johnson and kept Jack's *Some Of The Dharma* beside my bed in the lush new Penguin edition. Finally, Richard Zoglin's *Elvis In Vegas* brought vividly to life the thrill of Elvis's first comeback show at The International.

LIKE FIRE UNBOUND

"A slow burn in its purest form –
Petherick's fiery prose evokes a city
smouldering with impassioned tensions
that build towards an incendiary
denouncement." – JAKE ARNOTT,
AUTHOR OF *THE LONG FIRM*

A disparate cast of characters are drawn together
under the gaze of a mysterious mystic as they
try their best to survive in the new contemporary
capital, a city of changing rules, privatised streets,
gig economies, fractured traditions.

As the heat beats down upon them, day after day,
they each attempt differing strategies to maintain
their place, to protect their futures and somehow to
forge a way through the challenge of the day. And in
the background is the story of Lily Cadyman, maid
to Thomas Farriner, whose bakery in Pudding Lane
was the source of the first flames which caused the
Great Fire of 1666.

"Petherick's London is fascinating and engaging. His
writing borders on the breathtaking."
– JOHN BIRD, FOUNDER OF *THE BIG ISSUE*

ENGLISH ARCADIA

"A spellbinding story that skilfully charts the disintegration of three generations of an English family following a horrific event at the bottom of an idyllic English garden. I was gripped from the first page."
– MICHAEL RIDPATH, AUTHOR OF *THE WANDERER*

In June 2017, after a self-imposed absence of twenty-five years, Darius Frome returns to the family home, an imposing Lutyens mansion towering above the Thames in Buckinghamshire. The grandson of maverick political aristocrat Sir Zachary Frome and his successful novelist wife Felicity Drummond, Darius is unsettled to discover the house of his childhood riven with discord.

Spanning a century of idealistic left-wing aspiration, *English Arcadia* delves into the depths of family rivalry, political ambition and personal tragedy, set against ancient themes of the natural world.

THE DAMNATION
OF PETER PAN

A dark and unsettling story of one
family's blighted relationship with JM
Barrie's most famous creation.

Peter Mannering, the 75-year-old
son of Maimie, one of the characters
featured in Barrie's novel *The Little
White Bird*, reflects on a life of wealth,
misfortune and violence. Demons summoned from
the past combine to present an horrific foretaste
of the future, yet down in the basement of his
Kensington mansion, a new generation of the family
surely offers the possibility of redemption?

Ranging from the sweet green hills of Laugharne,
the Welsh town made famous by Dylan Thomas, to
the frenetic life of Soho and the new pop culture of
the 1960s, *The Damnation Of Peter Pan* tells the story
of the twentieth century through a prism of love,
literature and the lexicon of the occult.

THE LAST
GOOD MAN

A novel of mystery, passion, loss
and longing set on a wild Cornish beach.

"The novel speaks eloquently
for itself...love, certainty, longing,
regret, survival. The story features
all that and more." – *DAILY MAIL*

"A searing story of love, loneliness and tragedy...
powerful plotline and stark imagery...descriptions
are deeply evocative of the beautiful yet often
savage coastal landscapes." – *CORNWALL TODAY*

A man has lived on his own beside the sea for
many years. From a choice made long ago, he keeps
himself separate from the world of people, and is
completely at one with his environment.

His solitude is broken by the discovery, one early
morning on the flat sands of a low tide, of a child
washed up on the beach.